FROGGY GOES TO SCHOO

FROGGY GOES TO SCHOOL

by JONATHAN LONDON
illustrated by FRANK REMKIEWICZ

SCHOLASTIC INC.
New York Toronto London Auckland Sydney

This one is for the teachers—
their patience, patience, patience.
—J. L.

For Sarah and the Roadrunners
—F. R.

ISBN 0-590-06693-5

12 11 10 9 8 7 6 5 4 3 2   4 5 6 / 0

Printed in the U.S.A.   08

First Scholastic printing, September 1997

It was the first day of school.
Froggy woke up
and looked out the window.
The sun was high in the sky.
"Oh no! The bus! The bus!" he cried.
"I'll miss the bus!"

He hopped out of bed

and flopped outside—*flop flop flop.*

The school bus was leaving.
"Wait! Wait!" he yelled,
and took a mighty hop.

The bus hissed to a stop
and the door folded open.
Froggy flopped up the steps—*flop flop flop*—
but when he reached the top
everybody laughed
and pointed their fingers.

"Wha-a-a-t?"
"Did you forget something?"
Froggy looked down.
"Oops!" He was in his *underwear!*

He dashed to the back of the bus
and hid behind Max's umbrella
all the way to school.

At school, he hopped behind bushes.

He tried to hide behind the flagpole.

He rolled down the hall
like a bowling ball.

And in class, he pretended
to be a flowerpot.

FRRROOGGYY! called his teacher. "Wha-a-a-t?" But it wasn't his teacher at all— it was his father!

Froggy rubbed his eyes.
He had been dreaming.
He was still in bed!
"Rise and shine, Froggy," said his father.
"It's the first day of school!"

This time Froggy got *all* dressed—
zip! zoop! zup!
zut! zut! zut! zat!
Then he flopped into the kitchen—
flop flop flop.

He tried to pour milk on his bowl of flies,
but the carton flew out of his hands.
"You're just nervous about school, Froggy,"
said his mother. "*Everybody* is, the first day."
"Not me!" cried Froggy.

And together they leapfrogged
all the way to the bus stop—*flop flop flop.*

At school, Froggy found
his name tag on his table.

He liked his name.
It was the first word
he knew how to read.

It was the only word
he knew how to read.

He read it aloud, louder and louder.

FRRROOGGYY!

cried his teacher, Miss Witherspoon.

"Wha-a-a-a-at?"
"Hush, dear. It's time to pay attention."

But it was hard to pay attention.
He squirmed.

He looked out the window
at the falling leaves.
He felt like a leaf,
falling . . . falling . . .

PLOP! He fell out of his chair. "Oops!"
"Kindly stay in your seat, dear,"
said Miss Witherspoon.
"We'll sit on the floor at circle time."

At circle time, Miss Witherspoon said,
"Now children, today I'd like you to tell us
what you did last summer.
Who wants to go first?"
Froggy shouted, "Me me me me me!"
and so did Max.
Miss Witherspoon went
clap   clap   clap clap clap—
and everybody went
clap   clap   clap clap clap with her.
Then they grew very quiet.
"Now one at a time,"
said Miss Witherspoon.

When Froggy's turn came,
he jumped up and said,
"Last summer, I learned how to swim!"
And he sang, "Bubble bubble, toot toot.
Chicken, airplane, soldier."

Everybody jumped up and joined in—
"Bubble bubble, toot toot.
Chicken, airplane, soldier"—

when—*uh-oh*—in walked the principal, Mr. Mugwort.
"Bubble bubble—*oops!*" cried Froggy,
looking more red in the face than green.
Mr. Mugwort glared at him . . .

then he joined in—
"Bubble bubble, toot toot.
Chicken, airplane, soldier"—
till the bell rang for recess.

When Froggy flopped off the bus after school,
his father said, "Froggy!
How was your first day of school?"
"Great!" said Froggy.
"I taught the principal how to swim!"

all the way home—*flop flop flop.*

"Hmmmmm, that's nice," said his mother,
"but where's your lunch box and baseball cap?"
"Oops! I left them at school."
"Oh, Froggy. Will you ever *learn?*" said his mother.
"That's why I'm going to *school,* Mom!"
And together they leapfrogged